Edgar Allan Poe's

Amusing Tales

A Collection of Short Stories

British Library Cataloguing-in-Publication Data
A catalogue record for this book is available from the
British Library

Contents

Edgar Allan Poe 4

Bon-Bon (1835) 7
The Business Man (1843) 31
The Angel of the Odd (1844) 46
X-Ing a Paragrab (1849) 62
Never Bet the Devil Your Head (1850) 72

Edgar Allan Poe

Edgar Allan Poe was born in Boston, Massachusetts in 1809. He was left an orphan at a very young age, following the abscondence of his father and subsequent death of his mother, but was taken in by a couple from Richmond, Virginia. After a brief spell living in England and Scotland, Poe enrolled at the newly-established University of Virginia. However, after just one semester, having become estranged from his foster father due to gambling debts, and finding himself unable to fund his studies, he dropped out. In 1827, aged 18, Poe travelled back to Boston, the city of his birth.

By now in severe financial trouble, Poe lied about his age in order to enlist in the army. After spending two years posted to South Carolina, and having failed as an officer's cadet at West Point, Poe left the military by getting deliberately court-martialled. He left for New York in 1831, where he released his third collection of poems, the first two having received almost zero attention. Not long after its publication, in March of 1831, Poe returned to Baltimore.

From 1831 onwards, Poe began in earnest to try and make a living as a writer, and turned from poetry to prose. Despite often finding himself penniless, and frequently having to move city to stay in employment as a critic, during the thirties and forties Poe published a good amount of fiction. Most of his best known short-stories, such as 'The Tell Tale Heart,' 'Ligeia', 'William Wilson' and 'The Fall of the House of Usher', were published between 1835 and 1845. In January 1845, Poe published his poem 'The Raven', which – despite fact that he only received $9 for it – was a great success, turning him overnight into something of a household name.

Poe died in 1849, aged just 40. The circumstances were somewhat odd; he was found wandering the streets of Baltimore at five in the morning, delirious and wearing someone else's clothes, and he repeatedly cried out "Reynolds!" during the hours before his death. The cause of death remains a mystery, with everything from epilepsy to rabies cited. However, whatever the reason behind his unusual passing, Poe's legacy is a formidable one: He is seen today as one of the greatest practitioners of Gothic and detective fiction that ever lived, and popular culture is replete with references to him.

Bon-Bon

"Notre Gulliver" — *dit le Lord Bolinbroke* — *"a de telles fables."* — Voltaire.

That Pierre Bon-Bon was a Restaurateur of uncommon qualifications, no man who, during the reign of ——, frequented the little Câfe in the Cul-de-sac Le Febvre at Rouen, will, I imagine, feel himself at liberty to dispute. That Pierre Bon-Bon was, in an equal degree, skilled in the philosophy of that period is, I presume, still more especially undeniable. His Patés à la fois were beyond doubt immaculate — but what pen can do justice to his essays sur la Nature — his thoughts sur l'Ame — his observations sur l'Esprit? If his omelettes — if his fricandeaux were inestimable, what literateur of that day would not have given twice as much for an 'Idée de Bon-Bon' as for all the trash of all the 'Idées' of all the rest of the savants? Bon-Bon had ransacked libraries which no other man had ransacked — had read more than any other would have entertained a notion of reading — had understood more than any other would have conceived the possibility of understanding; and although, while he flourished, there were not wanting some authors at Rouen, to assert "that his dicta evinced neither the purity of the Academy, nor the depth of the Lyceum" — although, mark me, his doctrines were by no means very generally comprehended, still it did not follow that they were difficult of comprehension. It was, I think, on account of their entire self-evidency that many persons were led to consider them abstruse. It is to Bon-Bon — but let this go no farther — it is to Bon-Bon that Kant himself is mainly indebted for his metaphysics. The former was not indeed a Platonist, nor strictly speaking an Aristotelian — nor did he, like the modern Leibnitz, waste those precious hours which might be employed in the invention of a fricassée, or, facili gradu, the analysis of a sensation, in frivolous attempts at reconciling the obstinate oils and waters of ethical discussion. Not at all. Bon-Bon was Ionic. Bon-Bon was equally Italic. He reasoned a priori. He reasoned also a posteriori. His ideas were innate — or otherwise. He believed in George of Trebizond. He believed in Bossarion. Bon-Bon was emphatically a — Bon-Bonist.

I have spoken of the philosopher in his capacity of Restaurateur. I would not however have any friend of mine imagine that in fulfilling his hereditary duties in that line, our hero wanted a proper estimation of their dignity and importance. Far from it. It was impossible to say in which branch of his duplicate profession he took the greater pride. In his opinion the powers of the mind held intimate connection with the capabilities of the stomach. By this I do not mean to insinuate a charge of gluttony, or indeed any other serious charge to the prejudice of the metaphysician. If Pierre Bon-Bon had his failings — and what great man has not a thousand? — if Pierre Bon-Bon, I say, had his failings, they were failings of very little importance — faults indeed which in other tempers have often been looked upon rather in the light of virtues. As regards one of these foibles I should not have mentioned it in this history but for the remarkable prominency — the extreme alto relievo in which it jutted out from the plane of his general disposition. Bon-Bon could never let slip an opportunity of making a bargain.

Not that Bon-Bon was avaricious — no. It was by no means necessary to the satisfaction of the philosopher, that the bargain should be to his own proper advantage. Provided a trade could be effected — a trade of any kind, upon any terms, or under any circumstances, a triumphant smile was seen for many days thereafter to enlighten his countenance, and a knowing wink of the eye to give evidence of his sagacity.

At any epoch it would not be very wonderful if a humor so peculiar as the one I have just mentioned, should elicit attention and remark. At the epoch of our narrative, had this peculiarity not attracted observation, there would have been room for wonder indeed. It was soon reported that upon all occasions of the kind, the smile of Bon-Bon was wont to differ widely from the downright grin with which that Restauranteur would laugh at his own jokes, or welcome an acquaintance. Hints were thrown out of an exciting nature — stories were told of perilous bargains made in a hurry and repented of at leisure — and instances were adduced of unaccountable capacities, vague longings, and unnatural inclinations implanted by the author of all evil for wise purposes of his own.

The philosopher had other weaknesses — but they are scarcely worthy of our serious examination. For example, there are few men of extraordinary profundity who are found wanting in an inclination for the bottle. Whether this inclination be an exciting cause, or rather a valid proof of such profundity, it is impossible to say. Bon-Bon, as far as I can learn, did not think the subject adapted to minute investigation — nor do I. Yet in the indulgence of a propensity so truly classical, it is not to be supposed that the Restaurateur would lose sight of that intuitive discrimination which was wont to characterize, at one and the same time, his Essais and his Omelettes. With him Sauterne was to Medoc what Catullus was to Homer. He would sport with a syllogism in sipping St. Peray, but unravel an argument over Clos de Vougeot, and upset a theory in a torrent of Chambertin. In his seclusions the Vin de Bourgogne had its allotted hour, and there were appropriate moments for the Côtes du Rhone. Well had it been if the same quick sense of propriety had attended him in the peddling propensity to which I have formerly alluded — but this was by no means the case. Indeed, to say the truth, that trait of mind in the philosophic Bon-Bon did begin at length to assume a character of strange intensity and mysticism, and, however singular it may seem, appeared deeply tinctured with the grotesque diablerie of his favorite German studies.

To enter the little Café in the Cul-de-Sac Le Febvre was, at the period of our tale, to enter the sanctum of a man of genius. Bon-Bon was a man of genius. There was not a sous-cuisinier in Rouen, who could not have told you that Bon-Bon was a man of genius. His very cat knew it, and forbore to whisk her tail in the presence of the man of genius. His large water-dog was acquainted with the fact, and upon the approach of his master, betrayed his sense of inferiority by a sanctity of deportment, a debasement of the ears, and a dropping of the lower jaw not altogether unworthy of a dog. It is, however, true that much of this habitual respect might have been attributed to the personal appearance of the metaphysician. A distinguished exterior will, I am constrained to say, have its weight even with a beast; and I am willing to allow much in the outward man of the Restaurateur calculated to impress the imagination of the quadruped. There is a peculiar majesty about the atmosphere of the little great — if I may be permitted so equivocal an expression — which mere physical bulk alone will be found at all times inefficient in creating. If, however, Bon-Bon was barely three feet in height, and if his head was diminutively small, still it was impossible to behold the rotundity of his stomach without a sense of magnificence nearly bordering upon the sublime. In its size both dogs and men must have seen a type of his acquirements — in its immensity a fitting habitation for his immortal soul.

I might here — if it so pleased me — dilate upon the matter of habiliment, and other mere circumstances of the external metaphysician. I might hint that the hair of our hero was worn short, combed smoothly over his forehead, and surmounted by a conical-shaped white flannel cap and tassels — that his pea-green jerkin was not after the fashion of those worn by the common class of Restaurateurs at that day — that the sleeves were something fuller than the reigning costume permitted — that the cuffs were turned up, not as usual in that barbarous period, with cloth of the same quality and color as the garment, but faced in a more fanciful manner with the particolored velvet of Genoa — that his slippers were of a bright purple, curiously filagreed, and might have been manufactured in Japan, but for the exquisite pointing of the toes, and the brilliant tints of the binding and embroidery — that his breeches were of the yellow satin-like material called aimable — that his sky-blue cloak,resembling in form a dressing-wrapper, and richly bestudded all over with crimson devices, floated cavalierly upon his shoulders like a mist of the morning — and that his tout ensemble gave rise to the remarkable words of Benevenuta, the Improvisatrice of Florence, "that it was difficult to say whether Pierre Bon-Bon was indeed a bird of Paradise, or the rather a very Paradise of perfection."

I have said that "to enter the Café in the Cul de Sac Le Febvre was to enter the sanctum of a man of genius" — but then it was only the man of genius who could duly estimate the merits of the sanctum. A sign consisting of a vast folio swung before the entrance. On one side of the volume was painted a bottle — on the reverse a Paté. On the back were visible in large letters the words Æuvres de Bon-Bon. Thus was delicately shadowed forth the two-fold occupation of the proprietor.

Upon stepping over the threshold the whole interior of the building presented itself to view. A long, low-pitched room of antique construction was indeed all the accommodation afforded by the Café in the Cul-de-Sac Le Febre. In a corner of the apartment stood the bed of the metaphysician. An array of curtains, together with a canopy à la Gréque gave it an air at once classic and comfortable. In the corner diagonally opposite appeared, in direct and friendly communion, the properties of the kitchen and the bibliothéque. A dish of polemics stood peacefully upon the dresser. Here lay an oven-full of the latest ethics — there a kettle of duodecimo melanges. Volumes of German morality were hand and glove with the gridiron — a toasting fork might be discovered by the side of Eusebius — Plato reclined at his ease in the frying pan — and contemporary manuscripts were filed away upon the spit.

In other respects the Café de Bon-Bon might be said to differ little from the Cafés of the period. A gigantic fire-place yawned opposite the door. On the right of the fire-place an open cupboard displayed a formidable array of labelled bottles. There Mousseux, Chambertin, St. George, Richbourg, Bordeaux, Margaux, Haubrion, Leonville, Medoc, Sauterne, Bârac, Preignac, Grave, Lafitte, and St. Peray contended with many other names of lesser celebrity for the honor of being quaffed. From the ceiling, suspended by a chain of very long slender links, swung a fantastic iron lamp, throwing a hazy light over the room, and relieving in some measure the placidity of the scene.

It was here, about twelve o'clock one night, during the severe winter of ———, that Pierre Bon-Bon, after having listened for some time to the comments of his neighbors upon his singular propensity — that Pierre Bon-Bon, I say, having turned them all out of his house, locked the door upon them with a sacre Dieu, and betook himself in no very pacific mood to the comforts of a leather-bottomed arm-chair, and a fire of blazing faggots.

It was one of those terrific nights which are only met with once or twice during a century. The snow drifted down bodily in enormous masses, and the Café de Bon-Bon tottered to its very centre, with the floods of wind that, rushing through the crannies in the wall, and pouring impetuously down the chimney, shook awfully the curtains of the philosopher's bed, and disorganized the economy of his Paté-pans and papers. The huge folio sign that swung without, exposed to the fury of the tempest, creaked ominously, and gave out a moaning sound from its stanchions of solid oak.

I have said that it was in no very placid temper the metaphysician drew up his chair to its customary station by the hearth. Many circumstances of a perplexing nature had occurred during the day, to disturb the serenity of his meditations. In attempting Des Œufs à la Princesse he had unfortunately perpetrated an Omelette à la Reine — the discovery of a principle in Ethics had been frustrated by the overturning of a stew — and last, not least, he had been thwarted in one of those admirable bargains which he at all times took such especial delight in bringing to a successful termination. But in the chafing of his mind at these unaccountable vicissitudes, there did not fail to be mingled a degree of that nervous anxiety which the fury of a boisterous night is so well calculated to produce. Whistling to his more immediate vicinity the large black water-dog we have spoken of before, and settling himself uneasily in his chair, he could not help casting a wary and unquiet eye towards those distant recesses of the apartment whose inexorable shadows not even the red fire-light itself could more than partially succeed in overcoming.

Having completed a scrutiny whose exact purpose was perhaps unintelligible to himself, Bon-Bon drew closer to his seat a small table covered with books and papers, and soon became absorbed in the task of retouching a voluminous manuscript, intended for publication on the morrow.

"I am in no hurry, Monsieur Bon-Bon" — whispered a whining voice in the apartment.

"The devil!" — ejaculated our hero, starting to his feet, overturning the table at his side, and staring around him in astonishment.

"Very true" — calmly replied the voice.

"Very true! — what is very true? — how came you here?" — vociferated the metaphysician, as his eye fell upon something which lay stretched at full length upon the bed.

"I was saying" — said the intruder, without attending to Bon-Bon's interrogatories — "I was saying that I am not at all pushed for time — that the business upon which I took the liberty of calling is of no pressing importance — in short that I can very well wait until you have finished your Exposition."

"My Exposition! — there now! — how do you know — how came you to understand that I was writing an Exposition? — good God!"

"Hush!" — replied the figure in a shrill under tone; and arising quickly from the bed he made a single step towards our hero, while the iron lamp overhead swung convulsively back from his approach.

The philosopher's amazement did not prevent a narrow scrutiny of the stranger's dress and appearance. The outlines of a figure, exceedingly lean, but much above the common height, were rendered minutely distinct by means of a faded suit of black cloth which fitted tight to the skin, but was otherwise cut very much in the style of a century ago. These garments had evidently been intended a priori for a much shorter person than their present owner. His ankles and wrists were left naked for several inches. In his shoes, however, a pair of very brilliant buckles gave the lie to the extreme poverty implied by the other portions of his dress. His head was bare, and entirely bald, with the exception of the hinder part, from which depended a queue of considerable length. A pair of green spectacles, with side glasses, protected his eyes from the influence of the light, and at the same time prevented our hero from ascertaining either their color or their conformation. About the entire person there was no evidence of a shirt; but a white cravat, of filthy appearance, was tied with extreme precision around the throat, and the ends hanging down formally side by side, gave, although I dare say unintentionally, the idea of an ecclesiastic. Indeed, many other points both in his appearance and demeanor might have very well sustained a conception of that nature. Over his left ear he carried, after the fashion of a modern clerk, an instrument resembling the stylus of the ancients. In a breast-pocket of his coat appeared conspicuously a small black volume fastened with clasps of steel. This book, whether accidentally or not, was so turned outwardly from the person as to discover the words "Rituel Catholique" in white letters upon the back. His entire physiognomy was interestingly saturnine — even cadaverously pale. The forehead was lofty and deeply furrowed with the ridges of contemplation. The corners of the mouth were drawn down into an expression of the most submissive humility. There was also a clasping of the hands, as he stepped towards our hero — a deep sigh — and altogether a look of such utter sanctity as could not have failed to be unequivocally prepossessing. Every shadow of anger faded from the countenance of the metaphysician, as, having completed a satisfactory survey of his visiter's person, he shook him cordially by the hand, and conducted him to a seat.

There would however be a radical error in attributing this instantaneous transition of feeling in the philosopher to any one of those causes which might naturally be supposed to have had an influence. Indeed Pierre Bon-Bon, from what I have been able to understand of his disposition, was of all men the least likely to be imposed upon by any speciousness of exterior deportment. It was impossible that so accurate an observer of men and things should have failed to discover, upon the moment, the real character of the personage who had thus intruded upon his hospitality. To say no more, the conformation of his visiter's feet was sufficiently remarkable — there was a tremulous swelling in the hinder part of his breeches — and the vibration of his coat tail was a palpable fact. Judge then with what feelings of satisfaction our hero found himself thrown thus at once into the society of a — of a person for whom he had at all times entertained such unqualified respect. He was, however, too much of the diplomatist to let escape him any intimation of his suspicions, or rather — I should say — his certainty in regard to the true state of affairs. It was not his cue to appear at all conscious of the high honor he thus unexpectedly enjoyed, but by leading his guest into conversation, to elicit some important ethical ideas which might, in obtaining a place in his contemplated publication, enlighten the human race, and at the same time immortalize himself — ideas which, I should have added, his visiter's great age, and well known proficiency in the science of Morals might very well have enabled him to afford.

Actuated by these enlightened views our hero bade the gentleman sit down, while he himself took occasion to throw some faggots upon the fire, and place upon the now re-established table some bottles of the powerful Vin de Mousseux. Having quickly completed these operations, he drew his chair vis à vis to his companion's, and waited until he should open the conversation. But plans even the most skilfully matured are often thwarted in the outset of their application, and the Restaurateur found himself entirely nonplused by the very first words of his visiter's speech.

"I see you know me, Bon-Bon," — said he: — "ha! ha! ha! — he! he! he! — hi! hi! hi! — ho! ho! ho! — hu! hu! hu!" — and the devil, dropping at once the sanctity of his demeanor, opened to its fullest extent a mouth from ear to ear so as to display a set of jagged, and fang-like teeth, and throwing back his head, laughed long, loud, wickedly, and uproariously, while the black dog crouching down upon his haunches joined lustily in the chorus, and the tabby cat, flying off at a tangent stood up on end and shrieked in the farthest corner of the apartment.

Not so the philosopher: he was too much a man of the world either to laugh like the dog, or by shrieks to betray the indecorous trepidation of the cat. It must be confessed, however, that he felt a little astonishment to see the white letters which formed the words "Rituel Catholique " on the book in his guest's pocket momentarily changing both their color and their import, and in a few seconds in place of the original title, the words Regitre des Condamnés blaze forth in characters of red. This startling circumstance, when Bon-Bon replied to [page 696:] his visiter's remark, imparted to his manner an air of embarrassment which might not probably have otherwise been observable.

"Why, sir," — said the philosopher — "why, sir, to speak sincerely — I believe you are — upon my word — the d —— dest — that is to say I think — I imagine — I have some faint — some very faint idea — of the remarkable honor —— "

"Oh! — ah! — yes! — very well!" — interrupted his majesty — "say no more — I see how it is." And hereupon, taking off his green spectacles, he wiped the glasses carefully with the sleeve of his coat, and deposited them in his pocket.

If Bon-Bon had been astonished at the incident of the book, his amazement was now increased to an intolerable degree by the spectacle which here presented itself to view. In raising his eyes, with a strong feeling of curiosity to ascertain the color of his guest's, he found them by no means black, as he had anticipated — nor gray, as might have been imagined — nor yet hazel nor blue — nor indeed yellow, nor red — nor purple — nor white — nor green — nor any other color in the heavens above, or in the earth beneath, or in the waters under the earth. In short Pierre Bon-Bon not only saw plainly that his majesty had no eyes whatsoever, but could discover no indications of their having existed at any previous period, for the space where eyes should naturally have been, was, I am constrained to say, simply a dead level of cadaverous flesh.

It was not in the nature of the metaphysician to forbear making some inquiry into the sources of so strange a phenomenon, and to his surprise the reply of his majesty was at once prompt, dignified, and satisfactory.

"Eyes! — my dear Bon-Bon, eyes! did you say? — oh! ah! I perceive. The ridiculous prints, eh? which are in circulation, have given you a false idea of my personal appearance. Eyes!! — true. Eyes, Pierre Bon-Bon, are very well in their proper place — that, you would say, is the head — right — the head

of a worm. To you likewise these optics are indispensable —
yet I will convince you that my vision is more penetrating
than your own. There is a cat, I see, in the corner — a pretty
cat! — look at her! — observe her well. Now, Bon-Bon, do
you behold the thoughts — the thoughts, I say — the ideas
— the reflections — engendering in her pericranium?

There it is now! — you do not. She is thinking we admire
the profundity of her mind. She has just concluded that I am
the most distinguished of ecclesiastics, and that you are the
most superfluous of metaphysicians. Thus you see I am not
altogether blind: but to one of my profession the eyes you
speak of would be merely an incumbrance, liable at any time
to be put out by a toasting iron or a pitchfork. To you, I allow,
these optics are indispensable. Endeavor, Bon-Bon, to use
them well — my vision is the soul."

Hereupon the guest helped himself to the wine upon the
table, and pouring out a bumper for Bon-Bon, requested him
to drink it without scruple, and make himself perfectly at
home.

"A clever book that of yours, Pierre" — resumed his
majesty, tapping our friend knowingly upon the shoulder,
as the latter set down his glass after a thorough compliance
with this injunction.

"A clever book that of yours, upon my honor. It's a work
after my own heart. Your arrangement of matter, I think,
however, might be improved, and many of your notions
remind me of Aristotle. That philosopher was one of my most
intimate acquaintances. I liked him as much for his terrible

ill temper, as for his happy knack at making a blunder. There is only one solid truth in all that he has written, and for that I gave him the hint out of pure compassion for his absurdity. I suppose, Pierre Bon-Bon, you very well know to what divine moral truth I am alluding."

"Cannot say that I ——"

"Indeed! — why I told Aristotle that by sneezing men expelled superfluous ideas through the proboscis."

"Which is — hiccup! — undoubtedly the case" — said the metaphysician, while he poured out for himself another bumper of Mousseux, and offered his snuff-box to the fingers of his visiter."

"There was Plato too" — continued his majesty, modestly declining the snuff-box and the compliment — "there was Plato, too, for whom I, at one time, felt all the affection of a friend. You knew Plato, Bon-Bon? — ah! no, I beg a thousand pardons. He met me at Athens, one day, in the Parthenon, and told me he was distressed for an idea. I bade him write down that 'o nous estin augos.' He said that he would do so, and went home, while I stepped over to the Pyramids. But my conscience smote me for the lie, and hastening back to Athens, I arrived behind the philosopher's chair as he was inditing the 'augas.' Giving the gamma a fillip with my finger I turned it upside down. So the sentence now reads 'o nous estin aulos,' and is, you perceive, the fundamental doctrine of his metaphysics."

"Were you ever at Rome?" — asked the Restaurateur as he finished his second bottle of Mousseux, and drew from the closet a larger supply of Vin de Chambertin.

"But once, Monsieur Bon-Bon — but once. There was a time" — said the devil, as if reciting some passage from a book — 'there was an anarchy of five years during which the republic, bereft of all its officers, had no magistracy besides the tribunes of the people, and these were not legally vested with any degree of executive power' — at that time, Monsieur Bon-Bon — at that time only I was in Rome, and I have no earthly acquaintance, consequently, with any of its philosophy.'"*

"What do you think of Epicurus? — what do you think of — hiccup! — Epicurus?"

"What do I think of whom? " — said the devil in astonishment — "you cannot surely mean to find any fault with Epicurus! What do I think of Epicurus! Do you mean me, sir? — I am Epicurus. I am the same philosopher who wrote each of the three hundred treatises commemorated by Diogenes Laertes."

"That's a lie!" — said the metaphysician, for the wine had gotten a little into his head.

"Very well! — very well, sir! — very well indeed, sir" — said his majesty.

"That's a lie!" — repeated the Restaurateur dogmatically — "that's a — hiccup! — lie!"

"Well, well! have it your own way" — said the devil pacifically: and Bon-Bon, having beaten his majesty at an argument, thought it his duty to conclude a second bottle of Chambertin.

"As I was saying" — resumed the visiter — "as I was observing a little while ago, there are some very outré notions in that book of yours, Monsieur Bon-Bon. What, for instance, do you mean by all that humbug about the soul? Pray, sir, what is the soul?"

"The — hiccup! — soul" — replied the metaphysician, referring to his MS. "is undoubtedly" —

"No, sir!"

"Indubitably" —

"No, sir!"

"Indisputably" —

"No, sir!"

"Evidently" —

"No, sir!"

"Incontrovertibly" —

"No, sir!"

"Hiccup!" —

"No, sir!"

"And beyond all question a" —

"No, sir! the soul is no such thing." (Here the philosopher finished his third bottle of Chambertin.)

"Then — hic-cup! — pray — sir — what — what is it?"

"That is neither here nor there, Monsieur Bon-Bon," replied his majesty, musingly. "I have tasted — that is to say I have known some very bad souls, and some too — pretty good ones." Here the devil licked his lips, and, having unconsciously let fall his hand upon the volume in his pocket, was seized with a violent fit of sneezing.

24

His majesty continued.

"There was the soul of Cratinus — passable: — Aristophanes — racy: — Plato — exquisite: — not your Plato, but Plato the comic poet: your Plato would have turned the stomach of Cerberus — faugh! Then let me see! there were Nœvius, and Andronicus, and Plautus, and Terentius. Then there were Lucilius, and Catullus, and Naso, and Quintius Flaccus — dear Quinty! as I called him when he sung a seculare for my amusement, while I toasted him in pure good humor on a fork. But they want flavor these Romans. One fat Greek is worth a dozen of them, and besides will keep, which cannot be said of a Quirite. Let us taste your Sauterne."

Bon-Bon had by this time made up his mind to the nil admirari, and endeavored to hand down the bottles in question. He was, however, conscious of a strange sound in the room like the wagging of a tail. Of this, although extremely indecent in his majesty, the philosopher took no notice — simply kicking the black water-dog and requesting him to be quiet. The visiter continued.

"I found that Horace tasted very much like Aristotle — you know I am fond of variety. Terentius I could not have told from Menander. Naso, to my astonishment, was Nicander in disguise. Virgilius had a strong twang of Theocritus. Martial put me much in mind of Archilochus — and Titus Livy was positively Polybius and none other."

"Hic — cup!" — here replied Bon-Bon, and his majesty proceeded.

"But if I have a penchant, Monsieur Bon-Bon, — if I

have a penchant, it is for a philosopher. Yet let me tell you, sir, it is not every dev — I mean it is not every gentleman who knows how to choose a philosopher. Long ones are not good, and the best, if not carefully shelled, are apt to be a little rancid on account of the gall."

"Shelled!!"

"I mean taken out of the carcass."

"What do you think of a — hiccup! — physician?"

"Don't mention them! — ugh! ugh!" (Here his majesty retched violently.) "I never tasted but one — that rascal Hippocrates! — smelt of asafœtida — ugh! ugh! ugh! — caught a wretched cold washing him in the Styx — and after all he gave me the cholera morbus."

"The — hiccup! — wretch!" — ejaculated Bon-Bon — "the — hic-cup! — abortion of a pill-box!" — and the philosopher dropped a tear.

"After all" — continued the visiter — "after all, if a dev — if a gentleman wishes to live he must have more talents than one or two, and with us a fat face is an evidence of diplomacy."

"How so?"

"Why we are sometimes exceedingly pushed for provisions. You must know that in a climate so sultry as mine, it is frequently impossible to keep a spirit alive for more than two or three hours; and after death, unless pickled immediately, (and a pickled spirit is not good,) they will — smell — you understand, eh? Putrefaction is always to be apprehended when the spirits are consigned to us in the usual way."

"Hiccup! — hiccup! — good God! how do you manage?"

Here the iron lamp commenced swinging with redoubled violence, and the devil half started from his seat — however with a slight sigh he recovered his composure, merely saying to our hero in a low tone, "I tell you what, Pierre Bon-Bon, we must have no more swearing."

Bon-Bon swallowed another bumper, and his visiter continued.

"Why there are several ways of managing. The most of us starve: some put up with the pickle. For my part I purchase my spirits *vivente corpore,* in which case I find they keep very well."

"But the body! — hiccup! — the body!!!" — vociferated the philosopher, as he finished a bottle of Sauterne.

"The body, the body — well, what of the body? — oh! ah! I perceive. Why, sir, the body is not at all affected by the transaction. I have made innumerable purchases of the kind in my day, and the parties never experienced any inconvenience. There were Cain, and Nimrod, and Nero, and Caligula, and Dionysius, and Pisistratus, and — and a thousand others, who never knew what it was to have a soul during the latter part of their lives; yet, sir, these men adorned society. Why is'nt there A ——, now, whom you know as well as I? Is he not in possession of all his faculties, mental and corporeal? Who writes a keener epigram? Who reasons more wittily? Who —— but, stay! I have his agreement in my pocket-book."

Thus saying, he produced a red leather wallet, and took from it a number of papers. Upon some of these Bon-Bon caught a glimpse of the letters MACHI . . . . . ., MAZA . . ., RICH . . . . . , and the words CALIGULA and ELIZABETH. His majesty selected a narrow slip of parchment, and from it read aloud the following words:

"In consideration of certain mental endowments which it is unnecessary to specify; and in farther consideration of one thousand louisd'or , I, being aged one year and one month, do hereby make over to the bearer of this agreement all my right, title, and appurtenance in the shadow called my soul." (Signed) A . . . . .* (Here his majesty repeated a name which I do not feel myself justifiable in indicating more unequivocally.)

"A clever fellow that A . . . . ." — resumed he; "but like you, Monsieur Bon-Bon, he was mistaken about the soul. The soul a shadow truly! — no such nonsense, Monsieur Bon-Bon. The soul a shadow!! ha! ha! ha! — he! he! he! — hu! hu! hu! Only think of a fricasséed shadow!"

"Only think — hiccup! — of a f-r-i-c-a-s-s-e-e-d s-h-a-d-o-w!!" echoed our hero, whose faculties were becoming gloriously illuminated by the profundity of his majesty's discourse.

"Only think of a — hiccup! — fricasseed shadow!!! Now damme! — hiccup! — humph! — if I would have been such a — hiccup! — nincompoop. My soul, Mr. — humph!"

"Your soul, Monsieur Bon-Bon?"

"Yes, sir — hiccup! — my soul is" —

28

"What, sir! ?"

"No shadow, damme!"

"Did not mean to say" —

"Yes, sir, my soul is — hiccup! — humph! — yes, sir."

"Did not intend to assert" —

"My soul is — hiccup! — peculiarly qualified for — hiccup! — a" —

"What, sir?"

"Stew."

"Ha!"

"Souflée."

"Eh?"

"Fricassée."

"Indeed!"

"Ragout or Fricandeau — and I'll let you have it — hiccup! — a bargain."

"Could'nt think of such a thing," said his majesty calmly, at the same time arising from his seat. The metaphysician stared.

"Am supplied at present," said his majesty.

"Hiccup! — e-h?" — said the philosopher.

"Have no funds on hand."

"What! ?"

"Besides, very ungentlemanly in me" —

"Sir!"

"To take advantage of" —

"Hiccup!"

"Your present situation."

Here his majesty bowed and withdrew — in what manner the philosopher could not precisely ascertain — but in a well-concerted effort to discharge a bottle at "the villain," the slender chain was severed that depended from the ceiling, and the metaphysician prostrated by the downfall of the lamp.

The Business Man

Method is the soul of business. — Old Saying

I am a business man. I am a methodical man. Method is the thing, after all. But there are no people I more heartily despise than your eccentric fools who prate about method without understanding it; attending strictly to its letter, and violating its spirit. These fellows are always doing the most out-of-the-way things in what they call an orderly manner. Now here — I conceive it — is a positive paradox. True method appertains to the ordinary and the obvious alone, and cannot be applied to the outre. What definite idea can a body attach to such expressions as "a methodical Jack o' Dandy," or "a systematic Will o' the Wisp?"

My notions upon this head might not have been so clear as they are, nor should I have been so well to do in the world as I am, but for a fortunate accident which happened to me when I was a very little boy. A good-hearted old Irish nurse (whom I shall not forget in my will) took me up one day by my heels, when I was making more noise than was necessary, and swinging me round two or three times, blasted my eyes for "a skreeking little spalpeen," and then knocked my head into a cocked hat against the bed-post. This, I say, decided my fate, and made my fortune. A tremendous bump got up at once on my sinciput, and turned out to be as pretty an organ of order as one shall see on a summer's day. Hence that positive appetite for system and regularity which has made me the distinguished man of business that I am. If there is any thing on earth that I hate, it is a genius. Your geniusess [[geniuses]] are all arrant asses — the greater the genius the greater the ass — and to this rule there is no exception whatever. Especially, you cannot make a man of business out of a genius, any more than money out of a Jew, or the best nutmegs out of pine-knots. The creatures are always going off at a tangent into some fantastic employment, or ridiculous speculation, entirely at variance with the "fitness of things," and having no business whatever to be considered as a business at all. Thus you may tell these characters immediately by the nature of their occupations. If ever you perceive a man setting up as a merchant, or a manufacturer, or going into the cotton or tobacco trade, or any of those eccentric pursuits; or getting to be a dry goods dealer, or soap-boiler, or something of that kind; or pretending to be a lawer, a blacksmith, or a physician — any thing out of the usual way — if ever, in short, you see a conceited fellow running heels over head into the patent blacking, or linen draping, or dog-meat line, you may set him down at once as a genius, and then, according to the rule of three, he's an ass.

Now I am not in any respect a genius, but a regular business man. My Daybook and Ledger will evince this in a minute. They are all well kept, though I say it myself; and, in my general habits of accuracy and punctuality, I am not to be beaten by a clock. Moreover, my occupations have been always been made to chime in with the ordinary pursuits of my fellow men. Not that I feel the least indebted, upon this score, to my exceedingly weak-minded parents, who, beyond doubt, would have made an arrant genius of me at last, if my guardian angel had not come, in good time, to the rescue. In biography the truth is every thing, and in auto-biography it is especially so — yet I scarcely hope to be believed when I state, however solemnly, that my poor father put me, when I was about fifteen years of age, into the counting-house of what he termed "a respectable hardware and commission merchant, doing a capital bit of business!" A capital bit of fiddlestick! However, the consequence of this folly was, in two or three days, I had to be sent home to my button-headed family in a high state of fever, and with a most violent and dangerous pain in the sinciput, all round about my organ of order. It was nearly a gone case with me then — just touch and go for six weeks — the physicians giving me up, and all that sort of thing. But, although I suffered much, I was a thankful boy in the main. I was saved from being a "respectable hardware and commission merchant, doing a capital bit of business," and I felt grateful to the protuberance which had been the means of my salvation as well as to the kind-hearted female who had originally put these means within my reach.

The most of boys run away from home at ten or twelve years of age, but I waited till I was sixteen. I don't know that I should have even gone just then, if I had not happened to hear my old mother talking about setting me up on my own hook in the grocery way. The grocery way! — only think of that! I resolved to be off forthwith, and try and establish myself in some decent occupation, without dancing attendance any longer upon the caprices of these eccentric old people, and running the risk of being made a genius of in the end. In this project I succeeded perfectly well at the first effort, and, by the time I was fairly eighteen, found myself doing an extensive and profitable business in the Tailors' Walking Advertisement line.

I was enabled to discharge the onerous duties of this profession only by that rigid adherence to system which formed the leading feature of my mind. A scrupulous method characterised my actions, as well as my accounts. In my case, it was method — not money — which made the man: at least all of him that was not made by the tailor whom I served. At nine, every morning, I called upon that individual for the clothes of the day. Ten o'clock found me in some fashionable promenade, or other place of public amusement. The precise regularity with which I turned my handsome person about, so as to bring successively into view every portion of the suit upon my back, was the admiration of all the knowing men in the trade. Noon never passed without my bringing home a customer to the house of my employers, Messieurs Cut and Comeagain. I say this proudly, but with tears in my eyes — for the firm proved themselves the basest of ingrates. The little account about which we quarrelled and finally parted, cannot, in any item, be thought overcharged, by gentlemen really conversant with the nature of the business. Upon this point, however, I feel a degree of proud satisfaction in permitting the reader to judge for himself. My bill ran thus:

Messrs. Cut and Comeagain, Merchant Tailors.

To Peter Proffit, Walking Advertiser,   Drs.
July 10.

To promenade, as usual, and customer brought home,

$00 25
July 11.

To promenade, as usual, and customer brought home,

25
July 12.

To one lie, second class; damaged black cloth sold for invisible green,

25
July 13.

To one lie, first class, extra quality and size; recommending milled sattinet as broad-cloth,

75
July 20.

To purchasing bran new paper shirt collar or dickey, to set off gray Petersham,

2
Aug. 15.

To wearing double-padded bobtail frock, (thermometer 206 in the shade,)

25
Aug. 16.

To standing on one leg three hours, to show off new-touch strapped pants, at 12 ½ cts per leg, per hour,

37 ½
Aug. 17.

To promenade, as usual, and large customer brought home (fat man,)

50
Aug. 18.

To promenade, as usual, (medium size,)

25
Aug. 19.

To promenade, as usual, (small man and bad pay,)

6 ¼

———

$2 96 ¾

The item chiefly disputed in this bill was the very moderate charge of two pennies for the dickey. Upon my word of honor, this was not an unreasonable price for that dickey. It was one of the cleanest and prettiest little dickeys I ever saw; and I have good reason to believe that it effected the sale of three Petershams. The elder partner of the firm, however, would allow only one penny of the charge, and took it upon himself to show in what manner four of the same sized conveniences could be got out of a sheet of foolscap. But it is needless to say that I stood upon the principle of the thing. Business is business, and should be done in a business way. There was no system whatever in swindling me out of a penny — a clear fraud of fifty per cent. — no method in any respect. I left, at once, the employment of Messieurs, Cut and Comeagain, and set up in the Eye-Sore line by myself — one of the most lucrative, respectable, and independent of the ordinary occupations.

My strict integrity, economy, and rigorous business habits, here again came into play. I found myself driving a flourishing trade, and soon became a marked man upon 'Change.' The truth is, I never dabbled in flashy matters, but jogged on in the good old sober routine of the calling — a calling in which I should, no doubt, have remained to the present hour, but for a little accident which happened to me in the prosecution of one of the usual business operations of the profession. Whenever a rich old hunks, or prodigal heir, or bankrupt corporation, gets into the notion of putting up a palace, there is no such thing in the world as stopping either of them, and this every intelligent person knows. The fact in question, is indeed the basis of the Eye-Sore trade. As soon, therefore, as a building project is fairly afoot by one of these parties, we merchants secure a nice corner of the lot in contemplation, or a prime little situation just adjoining, or tight in front. — This done, we wait until the palace is half-way up, and then we pay some tasty architect to run us up an ornamental mud hovel right against it, or a Down East or Dutch Pagoda, or any ingenious little bit of fancy work, either Esquimaux, Kickapoo, or Hottentot. Of course, we can't afford to take these structures down under a bonus of five hundred per cent. upon the prime cost of our lot and plaster. Can we? I ask the question. I ask it of business men. It would be irrational to suppose that we can. And yet there was a rascally corporation which asked me to do this very thing — this very thing! I did not reply to their absurd proposition, of course; but I felt it a duty to go that same night, and lamp-

38

black the whole of their palace. For this, the unreasonable villains clapped me in jail; and the gentlemen of the Eye-Sore trade could not well avoid cutting my connexion when I came out.

The Assault and Battery business, into which I was now forced to adventure for a livelihood, was one somewhat ill adapted to the delicate nature of my constitution; but I went to work in it with a good heart, and found my account, here as heretofore, in those stern habits of methodical accuracy which had been thumped into me by that delightful old nurse — I would indeed be the basest of men not to remember her well in my will. By observing, as I say, the strictest system in all my dealings, and keeping a well regulated set of books, I was enabled to get over many serious difficulties, and, in the end, to establish myself very decently in the profession. The truth is, that few individuals in my line, did a snugger little business than I. I will just copy out a page or so of my day-book; and this will save me the necessity of blowing my own trumpet — a contemptible practice, of which no high-minded man will be guilty. Now, the day-book is a thing that don't lie.

"Jan. 1. — New Year's day. Met Snap in the street, groggy. Hem — he'll do. Met Gruff shortly afterwards, blind drunk. Mem — he'll answer, too. Entered both gentlemen in my Ledger, and opened a running account with each.

"Jan. 2. — Saw Snap at the Exchange, and went up and trod on his toe. Doubled his fist, and knocked me down. Good! — got up again. Some trifling difficulty with Bag, my attorney. I want the damages at a thousand, but he says that, for so simple a knock-down, we can't lay them at more than five hundred. Mem — must get rid of Bag — no system at all.

"Jan. 3. — Went to the theatre, to look for Gruff. Saw him sitting in a side box, in the second tier, between a fat lady and a lean one. Quizzed the whole set through an opera-glass, till I saw the fat lady blush and whisper to G. Went round, then, into the box, and put my nose within reach of his hand. Would'nt pull it — no go. Wiped it, and tried again — no go. Sat down then, and winked at the lean lady, when I had the high satisfaction of finding him lift me up by the nape of the neck, and fling me over into the pit. Neck dislocated, and right leg capitally splintered. — Went home in high glee, drank a bottle of champagne, and booked the young man for five thousand. Bag says it'll do.

"Feb. 15. — Compromised the case of Mr. Snap. Amount entered in Journal — fifty cents — which see.

"Feb. 16. — Cast by that villain Gruff, who made me a present of five dollars. Costs of suit, four dollars and twenty-five cents. Net profit — see Journal — seventy-five cents." Now, here is a clear gain, in a very brief period, of no less than one dollar and twenty five cents — this in the mere cases of Snap and Gruff; and I solemnly assure the reader, that these extracts are taken at random from my Day-Book.

It's an old saying, and a true one, however, that money is nothing in comparison with health. I found the exactions of the profession, somewhat too much, for my delicate state of body; and discovering, at last, that I was knocked out of all shape, so that I didn't know very well what to make of the matter, and my friends, when they met me in the street, couldn't tell that I was Peter Proffit at all, it occurred to me that the best expedient I could adopt was to alter my line of business. I turned my attention, therefore, to Mud-Dabbling, and continued it for some years.

The worst of this occupation, is, that too many people take a fancy to it, and the competition, is, in consequence, excessive. Every ignoramus of a fellow who finds that he hasn't brains in sufficient quantity to make his way as a walking-advertiser, or an eye-sore prig, or a salt and batter man, thinks of course, that he'll answer very well as a dabbler of mud. But there never was entertained a more erroneous idea that it requires no brains to mud-dabble. Especially, there is nothing to be made in this way without method. I did only a retail business myself, but my old habits of system carried me swimmingly along. I selected my street-crossing, in the first place, with great deliberation, and I never put down a broom in any part of the town but that. I took care, too, to have a nice little puddle at hand which I could get at in a minute. By these means I got to be well known as a man to be trusted; and this is one-half the battle, let me tell you, in trade. Nobody ever failed to pitch me a copper, and got over my crossing with a clean pair of pantaloons. And, as my business habits, in this respect, were sufficiently understood, I never met with any attempt at imposition. I wouldn't have put up with it, if I had. Never imposing upon any one myself, I suffered no one to play the possum with me. The frauds of the banks, I couldn't of course help. Their suspension put me to ruinous inconvenience. These, however, are not individuals, but corporations; and corporations, it is very well known, have neither bodies to be kicked, nor souls to be lost.

I was making money at this business, when, in an evil moment, I was induced to merge it in the Cur-Spattering — a somewhat analogous, but by no means so respectable a profession. My location, to be sure, was an excellent one, being central, and I had capital blacking and brushes. My little dog, too, was quite fat, and up to all varieties of snuff. He had been in the trade a long time, and, I may say, understood it. Our general routine was this: Pompey, having rolled himself well in the mud, sat upon end at the shop-door, until he observed a dandy approaching in bright boots. He then proceeded to meet him, and gave the Wellingtons a rub or two with his wool. Then the dandy swore very much, and looked about for a boot-black. There I was, full in his view, with blacking and brushes. It was only a minute's work, and then came a sixpence. This did moderately well for a time — in fact, I was not avaricious, but my dog was. I allowed him a third of the profits, but he was advised to insist upon half. This I could'nt stand — so we quarreled and parted.

I next tried my hand at the Organ-Grinding, for a while, and may say that I made out pretty well. It is a plain, straight-forward business, and requires no particular abilities. You can get a music-mill for a mere song, and, to put it in order, you have but to open the works, and give them three or four smart raps with a hammer. In improves the tone of the thing, for business purposes, more than you can imagine. This done you have only to stroll along, with the mill on your back, until you see tan-bark in the street, and a knocker wrapped up in buckskin. Then you stop and grind; looking as if you meant to stop and grind till doomsday. Presently a window opens, and somebody pitches you a sixpence, with a request to "hush up and go on," &c. I am aware that some grinders have actually afforded to "go on" for this sum; but for my part, I found my account in never going on under a shilling.

At this occupation I did a good deal; but, somehow, I was not quite satisfied, and so, finally, abandoned it. The truth is, I labored under the disadvantage of having no monkey — and streets are so muddy — and the populace are so impertinent with so many dirty little boys.

I was now out of employment for some months, but at length succeeded, by dint of great interest, in procuring a situation in the Sham-Post. The duties, here, are simple, and not altogether unprofitable. For example: — very early in the morning I had to make up my packet of sham-letters. Upon the inside of each of these I had to scrawl a few lines — on any subject which occurred to me as sufficiently mysterious — signing all the epistles Tom Dobson, or Toby Bobby Tompkins, or anything in that way. Having folded and sealed all, and stamped them with sham post-marks — New Orleans, Bengal, Botany Bay, or any other place a great way off — I set out, forthwith, upon my daily route, as if in a very great hurry. I always called at the big houses to deliver the letters, and receive the postage. Nobody hesitates at paying for a letter — especially for a double one — people are such fools — and it was no trouble, on my part, to get round a corner before there was time to open the epistles.

The worst of this profession, was, that I had to walk so much and so fast; and so frequently to vary my route. Besides, I had serious scruples of conscience. I can't bear to hear innocent individuals abused — and the way the whole town took to cursing Tom Dobson and Bobby Tompkins, was really awful to hear. I washed my hands of the matter in disgust.

My eighth and last speculation has been in the Cat-growing way. I have found that a most pleasant and lucrative business, and really, no trouble at all. The country, it is well known, has become infested with cats — so much so of late, that a petition for relief, most numerously and respectably signed, was brought before the legislature at its late memorable session. The assembly, at this epoch, was unusually well-informed, and, having passed many other wise and wholesome enactments, it crowned all with the Cat-Act. In its original form this law offered a premium for cat-heads, (fourpence a-piece,) but the Senate succeeded in amending the main clause, so as to substitute the word "tails " for "heads." This amendment was so obviously proper, that the House concurred in it nem. con.

As soon as the Governor had signed the bill, I invested my whole estate in the purchase of cats and kittens. At first I could only afford to feed them upon mice, (which are cheap,) but, I at length found it my best policy to give them mock-turtle. Their tails, at the legislature price, now bring me in a good income; for I have discovered a way, in which, by means of Macassar oil, I can force three crops in a year; and, somehow or other, the old cats get accustomed to the thing, and would rather have the appendages cut off than otherwise. I consider myself, therefore, a made man, and am bargaining for a country seat upon the Hudson.

The Angel of the Odd

An Extravaganza

IT was a chilly November afternoon. I had just consummated an unusually hearty dinner, of which the dyspeptic truffe formed not the least important item, and was sitting alone in the dining-room, with my feet upon the fender, and at my elbow a small table which I had rolled up to the fire, and upon which were some apologies for dessert, with some miscellaneous bottles of wine, spirit and liqueur. In the morning I had been reading Glover's "Leonidas," Wilkie's "Epigoniad," Lamartine's "Pilgrimage," Barlow's "Columbiad," Tuckermann's "Sicily," and Griswold's "Curiosities"; I am willing to confess, therefore, that I now felt a little stupid. I made effort to arouse myself by aid of frequent Lafitte, and, all failing, I betook myself to a stray newspaper in despair. Having carefully perused the column of "houses to let," and the column of "dogs lost," and then the two columns of "wives and apprentices runaway," I attacked with great resolution the editorial matter, and, reading it from beginning to end without understanding a syllable, conceived the possibility of its being Chinese, and so re-read it from the end to the beginning, but with no more satisfactory result. I was about throwing away, in disgust,

This folio of four pages, happy work
Which not even critics criticise,

when I felt my attention somewhat aroused by the paragraph which follows :

"The avenues to death are numerous and strange. A London paper mentions the decease of a person from a singular cause. He was playing at 'puff the dart,' which is played with a long needle inserted in some worsted, and blown at a target through a tin tube. He placed the needle at the wrong end of the tube, and drawing his breath strongly to puff the dart forward with force, drew the needle into his throat. It entered the lungs, and in a few days killed him."

Upon seeing this I fell into a great rage, without exactly knowing why. "This thing," I exclaimed, "is a contemptible falsehood -- a poor hoax -- the lees of the invention of some pitiable penny-a-liner -- of some wretched concoctor of accidents in Cocaigne. These fellows, knowing the extravagant gullibility of the age, set their wits to work in the imagination of improbable possibilities -- of odd accidents, as they term them; but to a reflecting intellect (like mine," I added, in parenthesis, putting my forefinger unconsciously to the side of my nose,) "to a contemplative understanding such as I myself possess, it seems evident at once that the marvelous increase of late in these 'odd accidents' is by far the oddest accident of all. For my own part, I intend to believe nothing henceforward that has anything of the 'singular' about it."

"Mein Gott, den, vat a vool you bees for dat !" replied one of the most remarkable voices I ever heard. At first I took it for a rumbling in my ears -- such as a man sometimes experiences when getting very drunk -- but, upon second thought, I considered the sound as more nearly resembling that which proceeds from an empty barrel beaten with a big stick; and, in fact, this I should have concluded it to be, but for the articulation of the syllables and words. I am by no means naturally nervous, and the very few glasses of Lafitte which I had sipped served to embolden me no little, so that I felt nothing of trepidation, but merely uplifted my eyes with a leisurely movement, and looked carefully around the room for the intruder. I could not, however, perceive any one at all.

"Humph !" resumed the voice, as I continued my survey, "you mus pe so dronk as de pig, den, for not zee me as I zit here at your zide."

Hereupon I bethought me of looking immediately before my nose, and there, sure enough, confronting me at the table sat a personage nondescript, although not altogether indescribable. His body was a wine-pipe, or a rum-puncheon, or something of that character, and had a truly Falstaffian air. In its nether extremity were inserted two kegs, which seemed to answer all the purposes of legs. For arms there dangled from the upper portion of the carcass two tolerably long bottles, with the necks outward for hands.

All the head that I saw the monster possessed of was one of those Hessian canteens which resemble a large snuff-box with a hole in the middle of the lid. This canteen (with a funnel on its top, like a cavalier cap slouched over the eyes) was set on edge upon the puncheon, with the hole toward myself; and through this hole, which seemed puckered up like the mouth of a very precise old maid, the creature was emitting certain rumbling and grumbling noises which he evidently intended for intelligible talk.

"I zay," said he, "you mos pe dronk as de pig, vor zit dare and not zee me zit ere; and I zay, doo, you mos pe pigger vool as de goose, vor to dispelief vat iz print in de print. 'Tiz de troof -- dat it iz -- eberry vord ob it."

"Who are you, pray ?" said I, with much dignity, although somewhat puzzled; "how did you get here ? and what is it you are talking about ?"

"Az vor ow I com'd ere," replied the figure, "dat iz none of your pizzness; and as vor vat I be talking apout, I be talk apout vat I tink proper; and as vor who I be, vy dat is de very ting I com'd here for to let you zee for yourzelf."

"You are a drunken vagabond," said I, "and I shall ring the bell and order my footman to kick you into the street."

"He ! he ! he !" said the fellow, "hu ! hu ! hu ! dat you

can't do."

"Can't do !" said I, "what do you mean ? -- I can't do what ?"

"Ring de pell ;" he replied, attempting a grin with his little villainous mouth.

Upon this I made an effort to get up, in order to put my threat into execution; but the ruffian just reached across the table very deliberately, and hitting me a tap on the forehead with the neck of one of the long bottles, knocked me back into the arm-chair from which I had half arisen. I was utterly astounded; and, for a moment, was quite at a loss what to do. In the meantime, he continued his talk.

"You zee," said he, "it iz te bess vor zit still; and now you shall know who I pe. Look at me ! zee ! I am te Angel ov te Odd."

"And odd enough, too," I ventured to reply; "but I was always under the impression that an angel had wings."

"Te wing !" he cried, highly incensed, "vat I pe do mit te wing ? Mein Gott ! do you take me vor a shicken ?"

"No -- oh no !" I replied, much alarmed, "you are no chicken -- certainly not."

"Well, den, zit still and pehabe yourself, or I'll rap you again mid me vist. It iz te shicken ab te wing, und te owl ab te wing, und te imp ab te wing, und te head-teuffel ab te wing. Te angel ab not te wing, and I am te Angel ov te Odd."

"And your business with me at present is -- is" --

"My pizzness !" ejaculated the thing, "vy vat a low bred buppy you mos pe vor to ask a gentleman und an angel apout his pizziness !"

This language was rather more than I could bear, even from an angel; so, plucking up courage, I seized a salt-cellar which lay within reach, and hurled it at the head of the intruder. Either he dodged, however, or my aim was inaccurate; for all I accomplished was the demolition of the crystal which protected the dial of the clock upon the mantel-piece. As for the Angel, he evinced his sense of my assault by giving me two or three hard consecutive raps upon the forehead as before. These reduced me at once to submission, and I am almost ashamed to confess that either through pain or vexation, there came a few tears into my eyes.

"Mein Gott !" said the Angel of the Odd, apparently much softened at my distress; "mein Gott, te man is eder ferry dronk or ferry zorry. You mos not trink it so strong -- you mos put te water in te wine. Here, trink dis, like a goot veller, und don't gry now -- don't !"

Hereupon the Angel of the Odd replenished my goblet (which was about a third full of Port) with a colorless fluid that he poured from one of his hand bottles. I observed that these bottles had labels about their necks, and that these labels were inscribed "Kirschenwasser."

The considerate kindness of the Angel mollified me in no little measure; and, aided by the water with which he diluted my Port more than once, I at length regained sufficient temper to listen to his very extraordinary discourse. I cannot pretend to recount all that he told me, but I gleaned from what he said that he was the genius who presided over the contretemps of mankind, and whose business it was to bring about the odd accidents which are continually astonishing the skeptic. Once or twice, upon my venturing to express my total incredulity in respect to his pretensions, he grew very angry indeed, so that at length I considered it the wiser policy to say nothing at all, and let him have his own way. He talked on, therefore, at great length, while I merely leaned back in my chair with my eyes shut, and amused myself with munching raisins and filliping the stems about the room. But, by-and-by, the Angel suddenly construed this behavior of mine into contempt. He arose in a terrible passion, slouched his funnel down over his eyes, swore a vast oath, uttered a threat of some character which I did not precisely comprehend, and finally made me a low bow and departed, wishing me, in the language of the archbishop in Gil-Blas, "beaucoup de bonheur et un peu plus de bon sens."

His departure afforded me relief. The very few glasses of Lafitte that I had sipped had the effect of rendering me drowsy, and I felt inclined to take a nap of some fifteen or twenty minutes, as is my custom after dinner. At six I had an appointment of consequence, which it was quite indispensable that I should keep. The policy of insurance for my dwelling house had expired the day before; and, some dispute having arisen, it was agreed that, at six, I should meet the board of directors of the company and settle the terms of a renewal. Glancing upward at the clock on the mantel-piece, (for I felt too drowsy to take out my watch), I had the pleasure to find that I had still twenty-five minutes to spare. It was half past five; I could easily walk to the insurance office in five minutes; and my usual siestas had never been known to exceed five and twenty. I felt sufficiently safe, therefore, and composed myself to my slumbers forthwith.

Having completed them to my satisfaction, I again looked toward the time-piece and was half inclined to believe in the possibility of odd accidents when I found that, instead of my ordinary fifteen or twenty minutes, I had been dozing only three; for it still wanted seven and twenty of the appointed hour. I betook myself again to my nap, and at length a second time awoke, when, to my utter amazement, it still wanted twenty-seven minutes of six. I jumped up to examine the clock, and found that it had ceased running. My watch informed me that it was half past seven; and, of course, having slept two hours, I was too late for my appointment. "It will make no difference," I said : "I can call at the office in the morning and apologize; in the meantime what can be the matter with the clock ?" Upon examining it I discovered that one of the raisin stems which I had been filliping about the room during the discourse of the Angel of the Odd, had flown through the fractured crystal, and lodging, singularly enough, in the key-hole, with an end projecting outward, had thus arrested the revolution of the minute hand.

"Ah !" said I, "I see how it is. This thing speaks for itself. A natural accident, such as will happen now and then !"

I gave the matter no further consideration, and at my usual hour retired to bed. Here, having placed a candle upon a reading stand at the bed head, and having made an attempt to peruse some pages of the "Omnipresence of the Deity," I unfortunately fell asleep in less than twenty seconds, leaving the light burning as it was.

My dreams were terrifically disturbed by visions of the Angel of the Odd. Methought he stood at the foot of the couch, drew aside the curtains, and, in the hollow, detestable tones of a rum puncheon, menaced me with the bitterest vengeance for the contempt with which I had treated him. He concluded a long harangue by taking off his funnel-cap, inserting the tube into my gullet, and thus deluging me with an ocean of Kirschenwasser, which he poured, in a continuous flood, from one of the long necked bottles that stood him instead of an arm. My agony was at length insufferable, and I awoke just in time to perceive that a rat had ran off with the lighted candle from the stand, but not in season to prevent his making his escape with it through the hole. Very soon, a strong suffocating odor assailed my nostrils; the house, I clearly perceived, was on fire. In a few minutes the blaze broke forth with violence, and in an incredibly brief period the entire building was wrapped in flames. All egress from my chamber, except through a window, was cut off. The crowd, however, quickly procured and raised a long ladder. By means of this I was descending rapidly, and in apparent safety, when a huge hog, about whose rotund stomach, and indeed about whose whole air and physiognomy, there was something which reminded me of the Angel of the Odd, -- when this hog, I say, which hitherto had been quietly slumbering in the mud, took it suddenly into his head that his left shoulder needed scratching, and could find no more convenient rubbing-post than that afforded by the foot of the ladder. In an instant I was precipitated and had the misfortune to fracture my arm.

This accident, with the loss of my insurance, and with the more serious loss of my hair, the whole of which had been singed off by the fire, predisposed me to serious impressions, so that, finally, I made up my mind to take a wife. There was a rich widow disconsolate for the loss of her seventh husband, and to her wounded spirit I offered the balm of my vows. She yielded a reluctant consent to my prayers. I knelt at her feet in gratitude and adoration. She blushed and bowed her luxuriant tresses into close contact with those supplied me, temporarily, by Grandjean. I know not how the entanglement took place, but so it was. I arose with a shining pate, wigless ; she in disdain and wrath, half buried in alien hair. Thus ended my hopes of the widow by an accident which could not have been anticipated, to be sure, but which the natural sequence of events had brought about.

Without despairing, however, I undertook the siege of a less implacable heart. The fates were again propitious for a brief period; but again a trivial incident interfered. Meeting my betrothed in an avenue thronged with the élite of the city, I was hastening to greet her with one of my best considered bows, when a small particle of some foreign matter, lodging in the corner of my eye, rendered me, for the moment, completely blind. Before I could recover my sight, the lady of my love had disappeared -- irreparably affronted at what she chose to consider my premeditated rudeness in passing her by ungreeted. While I stood bewildered at the suddenness of this accident, (which might have happened, nevertheless, to any one under the sun), and while I still continued incapable of sight, I was accosted by the Angel of the Odd, who proffered me his aid with a civility which I had no reason to expect. He examined my disordered eye with much gentleness and skill, informed me that I had a drop in it, and (whatever a "drop" was) took it out, and afforded me relief.

I now considered it high time to die, (since fortune had so determined to persecute me,) and accordingly made my way to the nearest river. Here, divesting myself of my clothes, (for there is no reason why we cannot die as we were born), I threw myself headlong into the current; the sole witness of my fate being a solitary crow that had been seduced into the eating of brandy-saturated corn, and so had staggered away from his fellows. No sooner had I entered the water than this bird took it into its head to fly away with the most indispensable portion of my apparel. Postponing, therefore, for the present, my suicidal design, I just slipped my nether extremities into the sleeves of my coat, and betook myself to a pursuit of the felon with all the nimbleness which the case required and its circumstances would admit. But my evil destiny attended me still. As I ran at full speed, with my nose up in the atmosphere, and intent only upon the purloiner of my property, I suddenly perceived that my feet rested no longer upon terra-firma; the fact is, I had thrown myself over a precipice, and should inevitably have been dashed to pieces but for my good fortune in grasping the end of a long guide-rope, which depended from a passing balloon.

As soon as I sufficiently recovered my senses to comprehend the terrific predicament in which I stood or rather hung, I exerted all the power of my lungs to make that predicament known to the æronaut overhead. But for a long time I exerted myself in vain. Either the fool could not, or the villain would not perceive me. Meantime the machine rapidly soared, while my strength even more rapidly failed. I was soon upon the point of resigning myself to my fate, and dropping quietly into the sea, when my spirits were suddenly revived by hearing a hollow voice from above, which seemed to be lazily humming an opera air. Looking up, I perceived the Angel of the Odd. He was leaning with his arms folded, over the rim of the car ; and with a pipe in his mouth, at which he puffed leisurely, seemed to be upon excellent terms with himself and the universe. I was too much exhausted to speak, so I merely regarded him with an imploring air.

For several minutes, although he looked me full in the face, he said nothing. At length removing carefully his meerschaum from the right to the left corner of his mouth, he condescended to speak.

"Who pe you," he asked, "und what der teuffel you pe do dare ?"

To this piece of impudence, cruelty and affectation, I could reply only by ejaculating the monosyllable "Help !"

"Elp !" echoed the ruffian -- "not I. Dare iz te pottle -- elp yourself, und pe tam'd !"

With these words he let fall a heavy bottle of Kirschenwasser which, dropping precisely upon the crown of my head, caused me to imagine that my brains were entirely knocked out. Impressed with this idea, I was about to relinquish my hold and give up the ghost with a good grace, when I was arrested by the cry of the Angel, who bade me hold on.

"Old on !" he said; "don't pe in te urry -- don't. Will you pe take de odder pottle, or ave you pe got zober yet and come to your zenzes ?"

I made haste, hereupon, to nod my head twice -- once in the negative, meaning thereby that I would prefer not taking the other bottle at present -- and once in the affirmative, intending thus to imply that I was sober and had positively come to my senses. By these means I somewhat softened the Angel.

"Und you pelief, ten," he inquired, "at te last ? You pelief, ten, in te possibilty of te odd ?"

I again nodded my head in assent.

"Und you ave pelief in me, te Angel of te Odd ?"

I nodded again.

"Und you acknowledge tat you pe te blind dronk and te vool ?"

I nodded once more.

"Put your right hand into your left hand preeches pocket, ten, in token ov your vull zubmizzion unto te Angel ov te Odd."

This thing, for very obvious reasons, I found it quite impossible to do. In the first place, my left arm had been broken in my fall from the ladder, and, therefore, had I let go my hold with the right hand, I must have let go altogether. In the second place, I could have no breeches until I came across the crow. I was therefore obliged, much to my regret, to shake my head in the negative -- intending thus to give the Angel to understand that I found it inconvenient, just at that moment, to comply with his very reasonable demand ! No sooner, however, had I ceased shaking my head than --

"Go to der teuffel, ten !" roared the Angel of the Odd.

In pronouncing these words, he drew a sharp knife across the guide-rope by which I was suspended, and as we then happened to be precisely over my own house, (which, during my peregrinations, had been handsomely rebuilt,) it so occurred that I tumbled headlong down the ample chimney and alit upon the dining-room hearth.

Upon coming to my senses, (for the fall had very thoroughly stunned me,) I found it about four o'clock in the morning. I lay outstretched where I had fallen from the balloon. My head grovelled in the ashes of an extinguished fire, while my feet reposed upon the wreck of a small table, overthrown, and amid the fragments of a miscellaneous dessert, intermingled with a newspaper, some broken glass and shattered bottles, and an empty jug of the Schiedam Kirschenwasser. Thus revenged himself the Angel of the Odd.

X-Ing a Paragrab

As it is well known that the 'wise men' came 'from the East,' and as Mr. Touch-and-go Bullet-head came from the East, it follows that Mr. Bullet-head was a wise man; and if collateral proof of the matter be needed, here we have it — Mr. B. was an editor. Irascibility was his sole foible; for in fact the obstinacy of which men accused him was anything but his foible, since he justly considered it his forte. It was his strong point — his virtue; and it would have required all the logic of a Brownson to convince him that it was 'anything else.'

I have shown that Touch-and-go Bullet-head was a wise man; and the only occasion on which he did not prove infallible, was when, abandoning that legitimate home for all wise men, the East, he migrated to the city of Alexander-the-Great-o-nopolis, or some place of a similar title, out West.

I must do him the justice to say, however, that when he made up his mind finally to settle in that town, it was under the impression that no newspaper, and consequently no editor, existed in that particular section of the country. In establishing 'The Tea-Pot,' he expected to have the field all to himself. I feel confident he never would have dreamed of taking up his residence in Alexander-the-Great-o-nopolis, had he been aware that, in Alexander-the-Great-o-nopolis, there lived a gentleman named John Smith (if I rightly remember), who, for many years, had there quietly grown fat in editing and publishing the 'Alexander-the-

Great-o-nopolis Gazette.' It was solely, therefore, on account of having been misinformed, that Mr. Bullet-head found himself in Alex —— suppose we call it Nopolis, 'for short' — but, as he did find himself there, he determined to keep up his character for obst — for firmness, and remain. So remain he did; and he did more; he unpacked his press, type, etc., etc., rented an office exactly opposite to that of the 'Gazette,' and, on the third morning after his arrival, issued the first number of 'The Alexan'— that is to say, of 'The Nopolis Tea-Pot:' — as nearly as I can recollect, this was the name of the new paper.

The leading article, I must admit, was brilliant — not to say severe. It was especially bitter about things in general — and as for the editor of 'The Gazette,' he was torn all to pieces in particular. Some of Bullet-head's remarks were really so fiery that I have always, since that time, been forced to look upon John Smith, who is still alive, in the light of a salamander. I cannot pretend to give all the 'Tea-pot's' paragraphs verbatim, but one of them run thus:

'Oh, yes! — Oh, we perceive! Oh, no doubt! The editor over the way is a genius — Oh, my! Oh, goodness, gracious! — what is this world coming to? Oh, tempora! Oh, Moses!'

A philippic at once so caustic and so classical, alighted like a bombshell among the hitherto peaceful citizens of Nopolis. Groups of excited individuals gathered at the corners of the streets. Every one awaited, with heartfelt anxiety, the reply of the dignified Smith. Next morning it appeared, as follows:

'We quote from "The Tea-Pot" of yesterday the subjoined

paragraph: — "Oh, yes! Oh, we perceive! Oh, no doubt! Oh, my! Oh, goodness! Oh, tempora! Oh, Moses!" Why, the fellow is all O! That accounts for his reasoning in a circle, and explains why there is neither beginning nor end to him, nor to anything that he says. We really do not believe the vagabond can write a word that hasn't an O in it. Wonder if this O-ing is a habit of his? By-the-by, he came away from Down-East in a great hurry. Wonder if he O's as much there as he does here? "O! it is pitiful? !'"

The indignation of Mr. Bullet-head at these scandalous insinuations, I shall not attempt to describe. On the eel-skinning principle, however, he did not seem to be so much incensed at the attack upon his integrity as one might have imagined. It was the sneer at his style that drove him to desperation. What! — he, Touch-and-go Bullet-head! — not able to write a word without an O in it! He would soon let the jackanapes see that he was mistaken. Yes! he would let him see how much he was mistaken, the puppy! He, Touch-and-go Bullet-head, of Frogpondium, would let Mr. John Smith perceive that he, Bullet-head, could indite, if it so pleased him, a whole paragraph — ay! a whole article — in which that contemptible vowel should not once — not even once — make its appearance. But no; — that would be yielding a point to the said John Smith. He, Bullet-head, would make no alteration in his style, to suit the caprices of any Mr. Smith in Christendom. Perish so vile a thought! The O forever! He would persist in the O. He would be as O-wy as O-wy could be.

Burning with the chivalry of this determination, the great Touch-and-go, in the next 'Tea-pot,' came out merely with this simple but resolute paragraph, in reference to this unhappy affair:

'The editor of the "Tea-pot" has the honor of advising the editor of "The Gazette" that he, (the "Tea-pot,") will take an opportunity, in to-morrow morning's paper, of convincing him, (the "Gazette,") that he, (the "Tea-pot,") both can and will be his own master as regards style: — he, (the "Tea-pot,") intending to show him, (the "Gazette,") the supreme, and indeed the withering contempt with which the criticism of him, (the "Gazette,") inspires the independent bosom of him, (the "Tea-pot,") by composing for the especial gratification (?) of him, (the "Gazette,") a leading article, of some extent, in which the beautiful vowel — the emblem of Eternity — yet so offensive to the hyper-exquisite delicacy of him, (the "Gazette,") shall most certainly not be avoided by his (the "Gazette's") most obedient, humble servant, the "Tea-pot." "So much for Buckingham!"'

In fulfilment of the awful threat thus darkly intimated rather than decidedly enunciated, the great Bullet-head, turning a deaf ear to all entreaties for 'copy,' and simply requesting his foreman to 'go to the d——l,' when he (the foreman) assured him (the 'Tea-pot') that it was high time to 'go to press:' turning a deaf ear to everything, I say, the great Bullet-head sat up until day-break, consuming the midnight oil, and absorbed in the composition of the really unparalleled paragraph, which follows:

'So ho, John! how now? Told you so, you know. Don't crow, another time, before you're out of the woods! Does your mother know you're out? Oh, no, no! — so go home at once, now, John, to your odious old woods of Concord! Go home to your woods, old owl, — go! You wont? Oh, poh, poh, John, don't do so! You've got to go, you know! So go at once, and don't go slow; for nobody owns you here, you know. Oh, John, John, if you don't go you're no homo — no! You're only a fowl, an owl; a cow, a sow; a doll, a Poll; a poor, old, good-for-nothing-to-nobody, log, dog, hog, or frog, come out of a Concord bog. Cool, N ow — cool! Do be cool, you fool! None of your crowing, old cock! Don't frown so — don't! Don't hollo, nor howl, nor growl, nor bow-wow-wow! Good Lord, John, how you do look! Told you so, you know — but stop rolling your goose of an old poll about so, and go and drown your sorrows in a bowl!'

Exhausted, very naturally, by so stupendous an effort, the great Touch-and-go could attend to nothing farther that night. Firmly, composedly, yet with an air of conscious power, he handed his MS. to the devil in waiting, and then, walking leisurely home, retired, with ineffable dignity, to bed.

Meantime the devil to whom the copy was entrusted, ran up stairs to his 'case,' in an unutterable hurry, and forthwith made a commencement at 'setting' the MS. 'up.'

In the first place, of course, — as the opening word was 'so' — he made a plunge into the capital S hole and came out in triumph with a capital S. Elated by this success, he immediately threw himself upon the little-o box with a

66

blind-fold impetuosity — but who shall describe his horror when his fingers came up without the anticipated letter in their clutch? who shall paint his astonishment and rage at perceiving, as he rubbed his knuckles, that he had been only thumping them, to no purpose, against the bottom of an empty box. Not a single little-o was in the little-o hole; and, glancing fearfully at the capital-O partition, he found that, to his extreme terror, in a precisely similar predicament. Awe-stricken, his first impulse was to rush to the foreman.

'Sir!' said he, gasping for breath, 'I can't never set up nothing without no o's.'

'What do you mean by that?' growled the foreman, who was in a very ill humor at being kept up so late.

'Why, sir, there beant an o in the office, neither a big un nor a little un!'

'What — what the d—l has become of all that were in the case?'

'I don't know, sir,' said the boy, 'but one of them ere G'zette devils is bin prowling bout here all night, and I spect he's gone and cabbaged em every one.'

'Dod rot him! I haven't a doubt of it,' replied the foreman, getting purple with rage — 'but I tell you what you do, Bob, that's a good boy — you go over the first chance you get and hook every one of their i's and (d—n them!) their izzards.'

'Jist so,' replied Bob, with a wink and a frown — 'I'll be into em, I'll let em know a thing or two; but in de meantime, that ere paragrab? Mus go in to-night, you know — else there'll be the d—l to pay, and —'

'And not a bit of pitch hot,' interrupted the foreman, with a deep sigh and an emphasis on the 'bit.' 'Is it a very long paragraph, Bob?'

'Shouldn't call it a wery long paragrab,' said Bob.

'Ah, well, then! do the best you can with it! we must get to press,' said the foreman, who was over head and ears in work; 'just stick in some other letter for o, nobody's going to read the fellow's trash, any how.'

'Wery well,' replied Bob, 'here goes it!' and off he hurried to his case; muttering as he went — 'Considdeble vell, them ere expressions, perticcler for a man as doesn't swar. So I's to gouge out all their eyes, eh? and d——n all their gizzards! Vell! this here's the chap as is jist able for to do it.' The fact is, that although Bob was but twelve years old and four feet high, he was equal to any amount of fight, in a small way.

The exigency here described is by no means of rare occurrence in printing-offices; and I cannot tell how to account for it, but the fact is indisputable, that when the exigency does occur, it almost always happens that x is adopted as a substitute for the letter deficient. The true reason, perhaps, is that x is rather the most superabundant letter in the cases, or at least was so in the old times —— long enough to render the substitution in question an habitual thing with printers. As for Bob, he would have considered it heretical to employ any other character, in a case of this kind, than the x to which he had been accustomed.

'I shell have to x this ere paragrab,' said he to himself, as he read it over in astonishment, 'but it's jest about the awfulest o

-wy paragrab I ever did see:' so x it he did, unflinchingly, and to press it went x-ed.

Next morning, the population of Nopolis were taken all aback by reading, in 'The Tea-pot,' the following extraordinary leader:

'Sx hx, Jxhn! hxw nxw? Txld yxu sx, yxu knxw. Dxn't crxw, anxther time, befxre yxu're xut xf the wxxds! Dxes yxur mxther knxw yxu're xut? Xh, nx, nx! sx gx hxme at xnce, nxw, Jxhn, tx yxur xdixus xld wxxds xf Cxncxrd! Gx hxme tx yxur wxxds, xld xwl, —— gx! Yxu wxnt? Xh, pxh, pxh, Jxhn, dxn't dx sx! Yxu've gxt tx gx, yxu knxw! sx gx at xnce and dxn't gx slxw; fxr nxbxdy xwns yxu here, yxu knxw. Xh, Jxhn, Jxhn, if yxu dxn't gx yxu're nx hxmx —— nx! Yxu're xnly a fxwl, an xwl; a cxw, a sxw; a dxll, a Pxll; a pxxr xld gxxd-fxr-nxthing-tx-nxbxdy lxg, dxg, hxg, xr frxg, cxme xut xf a Cxncxrd bxg. Cxxl, nxw —— cxxl! Dx be cxxl, yxu fxxl! Nxne xf yxur crxwing, xld cxck! Dxn't frxwn sx — dxn't! Dxn't hxllx, nxr hxwl, nxr grxwl, nxr bxw-wxw-wxw! Gxxd Lxrd, Jxhn, hxw yxu dx lxxk! Txld yxu sx, yxu knxw, but stxp rxlling yxur gxxse xf an xld pxll abxut sx, and gx and drxwn yxur sxrrxws in a bxwl!'

The uproar occasioned by this mystical and cabalistical article, is not to be conceived. The first definite idea entertained by the populace was, that some diabolical treason lay concealed in the hieroglyphics; and there was a general rush to Bullet-head's residence, for the purpose of riding him on a rail; but that gentleman was nowhere to be found. He had vanished, no one could tell how; and not even the ghost of him has ever been seen since.

Unable to discover its legitimate object, the popular fury at length subsided; leaving behind it, by way of sediment, quite a medley of opinion about this unhappy affair.

One gentleman thought the whole an X-ellent joke.

Another said that, indeed, Bullet-head had shown much X-uberance of fancy.

'A third admitted him X-entric, but no more.

A fourth could only suppose it the Yankee's design to X-press, in a general way, his X-asperation.

'Say, rather, to set an X-ample to posterity,' suggested a fifth.

That Bullet-head had been driven to an X-tremity, was clear to all; and in fact, since that editor could not be found, there was some talk about lynching the other one.

The more common conclusion, however, was that the affair was, simply, X-traordinary and in-X-plicable. Even the town mathematician confessed that he could make nothing of so dark a problem. X, everybody knew, was an unknown quantity; but in this case (as he properly observed), there was an unknown quantity of X.

The opinion of Bob, the devil (who kept dark 'about his having 'X-ed the paragrab'), did not meet with so much attention as I think it deserved, although it was very openly and very fearlessly expressed. He said that, for his part, he had no doubt about the matter at all, that it was a clear case, that 'Mr. Bullet-head never vould be persvaded fur to drink like other folks, but vas con tinually a-svigging o' that ere blessed XXX ale, and, as a naiteral consekvence, it jist puffed him up savage, and made him X (cross) in the X-treme.'

Never Bet the Devil Your Head

A Tale with a Moral

"CON tal que las costumbres de un autor," says Don Thomas de las Torres, in the preface to his "Amatory Poems" "sean puras y castas, importo muy poco que no sean igualmente severas sus obras" -- meaning, in plain English, that, provided the morals of an author are pure personally, it signifies nothing what are the morals of his books. We presume that Don Thomas is now in Purgatory for the assertion. It would be a clever thing, too, in the way of poetical justice, to keep him there until his "Amatory Poems" get out of print, or are laid definitely upon the shelf through lack of readers. Every fiction should have a moral; and, what is more to the purpose, the critics have discovered that every fiction has. Philip Melanchthon, some time ago, wrote a commentary upon the "Batrachomyomachia," and proved that the poet's object was to excite a distaste for sedition. Pierre la Seine, going a step farther, shows that the intention was to recommend to young men temperance in eating and drinking. Just so, too, Jacobus Hugo has satisfied himself that, by Euenis, Homer meant to insinuate John Calvin; by Antinous, Martin Luther; by the Lotophagi, Protestants in general; and, by the Harpies, the Dutch. Our more modern Scholiasts are equally acute. These fellows demonstrate a hidden meaning in "The Antediluvians," a parable in Powhatan," new views in "Cock Robin," and transcendentalism in "Hop O' My Thumb." In short, it has been shown that no man can sit down to write without a very profound design. Thus to authors in general much trouble is spared. A novelist, for example, need have no care of his moral. It is there -- that is to say, it is somewhere -- and the moral and the critics can take care of themselves. When the proper time arrives, all that the gentleman intended, and all that he did not intend, will be brought to light, in the "Dial," or the "Down-Easter," together with all that he ought to have intended, and the rest that he clearly meant to intend: -- so that it will all come very straight in the end.

There is no just ground, therefore, for the charge brought against me by certain ignoramuses -- that I have never written a moral tale, or, in more precise words, a tale with a moral. They are not the critics predestined to bring me out, and develop my morals: -- that is the secret. By and by the "North American Quarterly Humdrum" will make them ashamed of their stupidity. In the meantime, by way of staying execution -- by way of mitigating the accusations against me -- I offer the sad history appended, -- a history about whose obvious moral there can be no question whatever, since he who runs may read it in the large capitals which form the title of the tale. I should have credit for this arrangement -- a far wiser one than that of La Fontaine and others, who reserve the impression to be conveyed until the last moment, and thus sneak it in at the fag end of their fables.

Defuncti injuria ne afficiantur was a law of the twelve

tables, and De mortuis nil nisi bonum is an excellent injunction -- even if the dead in question be nothing but dead small beer. It is not my design, therefore, to vituperate my deceased friend, Toby Dammit. He was a sad dog, it is true, and a dog's death it was that he died; but he himself was not to blame for his vices. They grew out of a personal defect in his mother. She did her best in the way of flogging him while an infant -- for duties to her well -- regulated mind were always pleasures, and babies, like tough steaks, or the modern Greek olive trees, are invariably the better for beating -- but, poor woman! she had the misfortune to be left-handed, and a child flogged left-handedly had better be left unflogged. The world revolves from right to left. It will not do to whip a baby from left to right. If each blow in the proper direction drives an evil propensity out, it follows that every thump in an opposite one knocks its quota of wickedness in. I was often present at Toby's chastisements, and, even by the way in which he kicked, I could perceive that he was getting worse and worse every day. At last I saw, through the tears in my eyes, that there was no hope of the villain at all, and one day when he had been cuffed until he grew so black in the face that one might have mistaken him for a little African, and no effect had been produced beyond that of making him wriggle himself into a fit, I could stand it no longer, but went down upon my knees forthwith, and, uplifting my voice, made prophecy of his ruin.

The fact is that his precocity in vice was awful. At five

months of age he used to get into such passions that he was unable to articulate. At six months, I caught him gnawing a pack of cards. At seven months he was in the constant habit of catching and kissing the female babies. At eight months he peremptorily refused to put his signature to the Temperance pledge. Thus he went on increasing in iniquity, month after month, until, at the close of the first year, he not only insisted upon wearing moustaches, but had contracted a propensity for cursing and swearing, and for backing his assertions by bets.

Through this latter most ungentlemanly practice, the ruin which I had predicted to Toby Dammit overtook him at last. The fashion had "grown with his growth and strengthened with his strength," so that, when he came to be a man, he could scarcely utter a sentence without interlarding it with a proposition to gamble. Not that he actually laid wagers -- no. I will do my friend the justice to say that he would as soon have laid eggs. With him the thing was a mere formula -- nothing more. His expressions on this head had no meaning attached to them whatever. They were simple if not altogether innocent expletives -- imaginative phrases wherewith to round off a sentence. When he said "I'll bet you so and so," nobody ever thought of taking him up; but still I could not help thinking it my duty to put him down. The habit was an immoral one, and so I told him. It was a vulgar one- this I begged him to believe. It was discountenanced by society -- here I said nothing but the truth. It was forbidden by act of

Congress -- here I had not the slightest intention of telling a lie. I remonstrated -- but to no purpose. I demonstrated -- in vain. I entreated -- he smiled. I implored -- he laughed. I preached- he sneered. I threatened -- he swore. I kicked him -- he called for the police. I pulled his nose -- he blew it, and offered to bet the Devil his head that I would not venture to try that experiment again.

Poverty was another vice which the peculiar physical deficiency of Dammit's mother had entailed upon her son. He was detestably poor, and this was the reason, no doubt, that his expletive expressions about betting, seldom took a pecuniary turn. I will not be bound to say that I ever heard him make use of such a figure of speech as "I'll bet you a dollar." It was usually "I'll bet you what you please," or "I'll bet you what you dare," or "I'll bet you a trifle," or else, more significantly still, "I'll bet the Devil my head."

This latter form seemed to please him best; -- perhaps because it involved the least risk; for Dammit had become excessively parsimonious. Had any one taken him up, his head was small, and thus his loss would have been small too. But these are my own reflections and I am by no means sure that I am right in attributing them to him. At all events the phrase in question grew daily in favor, notwithstanding the gross impropriety of a man betting his brains like bank-notes: -- but this was a point which my friend's perversity of disposition would not permit him to comprehend. In the end, he abandoned all other forms of wager, and gave himself up to "I'll bet the Devil my head," with a pertinacity and exclusiveness of devotion that displeased not less than it surprised me. I am always displeased by circumstances for which I cannot account. Mysteries force a man to think, and so injure his health. The truth is, there was something in the air with which Mr. Dammit was wont to give utterance to his offensive expression -- something in his manner of enunciation -- which at first interested, and afterwards made me very uneasy -- something which, for want of a more definite term at present, I must be permitted to call queer; but which Mr. Coleridge would have called mystical, Mr. Kant pantheistical, Mr. Carlyle twistical, and Mr. Emerson hyperquizzitistical. I began not to like it at all. Mr. Dammits soul was in a perilous state. I resolved to bring all my eloquence into play to save it. I vowed to serve him as St. Patrick, in the Irish chronicle, is said to have served the toad, -- that is to say, "awaken him to a sense of his situation." I addressed myself to the task forthwith. Once more I betook myself to remonstrance. Again I collected my energies for a final attempt at expostulation.

When I had made an end of my lecture, Mr. Dammit indulged himself in some very equivocal behavior. For some moments he remained silent, merely looking me inquisitively in the face. But presently he threw his head to one side, and elevated his eyebrows to a great extent. Then he spread out the palms of his hands and shrugged up his shoulders. Then he winked with the right eye. Then he repeated the operation with the left. Then he shut them both up very tight. Then he opened them both so very wide that I became seriously alarmed for the consequences. Then, applying his thumb to his nose, he thought proper to make an indescribable movement with the rest of his fingers. Finally, setting his arms a-kimbo, he condescended to reply.

I can call to mind only the beads of his discourse. He would be obliged to me if I would hold my tongue. He wished none of my advice. He despised all my insinuations. He was old enough to take care of himself. Did I still think him baby Dammit? Did I mean to say any thing against his character? Did I intend to insult him? Was I a fool? Was my maternal parent aware, in a word, of my absence from the domiciliary residence? He would put this latter question to me as to a man of veracity, and he would bind himself to abide by my reply. Once more he would demand explicitly if my mother knew that I was out. My confusion, he said, betrayed me, and he would be willing to bet the Devil his head that she did not.

Mr. Dammit did not pause for my rejoinder. Turning upon his heel, he left my presence with undignified precipitation. It was well for him that he did so. My feelings had been wounded. Even my anger had been aroused. For once I would have taken him up upon his insulting wager. I would have won for the Arch-Enemy Mr. Dammit's little head -- for the fact is, my mamma was very well aware of my merely temporary absence from home.

But Khoda shefa midehed -- Heaven gives relief -- as the Mussulmans say when you tread upon their toes. It was in pursuance of my duty that I had been insulted, and I bore the insult like a man. It now seemed to me, however, that I had done all that could be required of me, in the case of this miserable individual, and I resolved to trouble him no longer with my counsel, but to leave him to his conscience and himself. But although I forebore to intrude with my advice, I could not bring myself to give up his society altogether. I even went so far as to humor some of his less reprehensible propensities; and there were times when I found myself lauding his wicked jokes, as epicures do mustard, with tears in my eyes: -- so profoundly did it grieve me to hear his evil talk.

*   *   *   *   *   *

One fine day, having strolled out together, arm in arm, our route led us in the direction of a river. There was a bridge, and we resolved to cross it. It was roofed over, by way of protection from the weather, and the archway, having but few windows, was thus very uncomfortably dark. As we entered the passage, the contrast between the external glare and the interior gloom struck heavily upon my spirits. Not so upon those of the unhappy Dammit, who offered to bet the Devil his head that I was hipped. He seemed to be in an unusual good humor. He was excessively lively -- so much so that I entertained I know not what of uneasy suspicion. It is not impossible that he was affected with the transcendentals. I am not well enough versed, however, in the diagnosis of this disease to speak with decision upon the point; and unhappily there were none of my friends of the "Dial" present. I suggest the idea, nevertheless, because of a certain species of austere Merry-Andrewism which seemed to beset my poor friend, and caused him to make quite a Tom-Fool of himself. Nothing would serve him but wriggling and skipping about under and over every thing that came in his way; now shouting out, and now lisping out, all manner of odd little and big words, yet preserving the gravest face in the world all the time. I really could not make up my mind whether to kick or to pity him. At length, having passed nearly across the bridge, we approached the termination of the footway, when our progress was impeded by a turnstile of some height. Through this I made my way quietly, pushing it around as usual. But this turn would not serve the turn of Mr. Dammit. He insisted upon leaping the stile, and said he could cut a pigeon-wing over it in the air. Now this, conscientiously speaking, I did not think he could do. The best pigeon-winger over all kinds of style was my friend Mr. Carlyle, and as I knew he could not do it, I would not believe that it could be done by Toby Dammit. I therefore told him, in so many words, that he was a braggadocio, and could not do what he said. For this I had reason to be sorry afterward; -- for he straightway offered to bet the Devil his head that he could.

I was about to reply, notwithstanding my previous resolutions, with some remonstrance against his impiety, when I heard, close at my elbow, a slight cough, which sounded very much like the ejaculation "ahem!" I started, and looked about me in surprise. My glance at length fell into a nook of the frame -- work of the bridge, and upon the figure of a little lame old gentleman of venerable aspect. Nothing could be more reverend than his whole appearance; for he not only had on a full suit of black, but his shirt was perfectly clean and the collar turned very neatly down over a white cravat, while his hair was parted in front like a girl's. His hands were clasped pensively together over his stomach, and his two eyes were carefully rolled up into the top of his head.

Upon observing him more closely, I perceived that he wore a black silk apron over his small-clothes; and this was a thing which I thought very odd. Before I had time to make any remark, however, upon so singular a circumstance, he interrupted me with a second "ahem!"

To this observation I was not immediately prepared to reply. The fact is, remarks of this laconic nature are nearly unanswerable. I have known a Quarterly Review non-plussed by the word "Fudge!" I am not ashamed to say, therefore, that I turned to Mr. Dammit for assistance.

"Dammit," said I, "what are you about? don't you hear? -- the gentleman says 'ahem!'" I looked sternly at my friend while I thus addressed him; for, to say the truth, I felt particularly puzzled, and when a man is particularly puzzled he must knit his brows and look savage, or else he is pretty sure to look like a fool.

"Dammit," observed I -- although this sounded very much like an oath, than which nothing was further from my thoughts -- "Dammit," I suggested -- "the gentleman says 'ahem!'"

I do not attempt to defend my remark on the score of profundity; I did not think it profound myself; but I have noticed that the effect of our speeches is not always proportionate with their importance in our own eyes; and if I had shot Mr. D. through and through with a Paixhan bomb, or knocked him in the head with the "Poets and Poetry of America," he could hardly have been more discomfited than when I addressed him with those simple words: "Dammit, what are you about?- don't you hear? -- the gentleman says 'ahem!'"

"You don't say so?" gasped he at length, after turning more colors than a pirate runs up, one after the other, when chased by a man-of-war. "Are you quite sure he said that? Well, at all events I am in for it now, and may as well put a bold face upon the matter. Here goes, then -- ahem!"

At this the little old gentleman seemed pleased -- God only knows why. He left his station at the nook of the bridge, limped forward with a gracious air, took Dammit by the hand and shook it cordially, looking all the while straight up in his face with an air of the most unadulterated benignity which it is possible for the mind of man to imagine.

"I am quite sure you will win it, Dammit," said he, with the frankest of all smiles, "but we are obliged to have a trial, you know, for the sake of mere form."

"Ahem!" replied my friend, taking off his coat, with a deep sigh, tying a pocket-handkerchief around his waist, and producing an unaccountable alteration in his countenance by twisting up his eyes and bringing down the corners of his mouth -- "ahem!" And "ahem!" said he again, after a pause; and not another word more than "ahem!" did I ever know him to say after that. "Aha!" thought I, without expressing myself aloud -- "this is quite a remarkable silence on the part of Toby Dammit, and is no doubt a consequence of his verbosity upon a previous occasion. One extreme induces another. I wonder if he has forgotten the many unanswerable questions which he propounded to me so fluently on the day when I gave him my last lecture? At all events, he is cured of the transcendentals."

"Ahem!" here replied Toby, just as if he had been reading my thoughts, and looking like a very old sheep in a revery.

The old gentleman now took him by the arm, and led him more into the shade of the bridge -- a few paces back from the turnstile. "My good fellow," said he, "I make it a point of conscience to allow you this much run. Wait here, till I take my place by the stile, so that I may see whether you go over it handsomely, and transcendentally, and don't omit any flourishes of the pigeon-wing. A mere form, you know. I will say 'one, two, three, and away.' Mind you, start at the word 'away'" Here he took his position by the stile, paused a moment as if in profound reflection, then looked up and, I thought, smiled very slightly, then tightened the strings of his apron, then took a long look at Dammit, and finally gave the word as agreed upon-

One -- two -- three -- and -- away!

Punctually at the word "away," my poor friend set off in a strong gallop. The stile was not very high, like Mr. Lord's -- nor yet very low, like that of Mr. Lord's reviewers, but upon the whole I made sure that he would clear it. And then what if he did not? -- ah, that was the question -- what if he did not? "What right," said I, "had the old gentleman to make any other gentleman jump? The little old dot-and-carry-one! who is he? If he asks me to jump, I won't do it, that's flat, and I don't care who the devil he is." The bridge, as I say, was arched and covered in, in a very ridiculous manner, and there was a most uncomfortable echo about it at all times -- an echo which I never before so particularly observed as when I uttered the four last words of my remark.

But what I said, or what I thought, or what I heard, occupied only an instant. In less than five seconds from his starting, my poor Toby had taken the leap. I saw him run nimbly, and spring grandly from the floor of the bridge, cutting the most awful flourishes with his legs as he went up. I saw him high in the air, pigeon-winging it to admiration just over the top of the stile; and of course I thought it an unusually singular thing that he did not continue to go over. But the whole leap was the affair of a moment, and, before I had a chance to make any profound reflections, down came Mr. Dammit on the flat of his back, on the same side of the stile from which he had started. At the same instant I saw the old gentleman limping off at the top of his speed, having caught and wrapt up in his apron something that fell heavily into it from the darkness of the arch just over the turnstile. At all this I was much astonished; but I had no leisure to think, for Dammit lay particularly still, and I concluded that his feelings had been hurt, and that he stood in need of my assistance. I hurried up to him and found that he had received what might be termed a serious injury. The truth is, he had been deprived of his head, which after a close search I could not find anywhere; so I determined to take him home and send for the homoeopathists. In the meantime a thought struck me, and I threw open an adjacent window of the bridge, when the sad truth flashed upon me at once. About five feet just above the top of the turnstile, and crossing the arch of the foot-path so as to constitute a brace, there extended a flat iron bar, lying with its breadth horizontally, and forming one of a series that served to strengthen the structure throughout its extent. With the edge of this brace it appeared evident that the neck of my unfortunate friend had come precisely in contact.

He did not long survive his terrible loss. The homoeopathists did not give him little enough physic, and what little they did give him he hesitated to take. So in the end he grew worse, and at length died, a lesson to all riotous livers. I bedewed his grave with my tears, worked a bar sinister on his family escutcheon, and, for the general expenses of his funeral, sent in my very moderate bill to the transcendentalists. The scoundrels refused to pay it, so I had Mr. Dammit dug up at once, and sold him for dog's meat.

Printed in Great Britain
by Amazon